'They'd just started back whe
sleeve and went "Ssssh!" They stopp

"What's up?"

"Listen!"

Sam listened. He heard a swishing, crackling noise. Something was pushing its way through the tangle, coming their way. He looked at Laura. "W-what is it?"

"Dunno." She looked around. A thick holly bush grew nearby. "Quick – behind that bush."

They'd just hidden themselves when a figure appeared, moving stealthily under the trees . . . '

Every morning on the way to school, twins Sam and Laura pass a creepy old house they have nicknamed *Dracula's Castle*. But what is the secret of the old house? And why is one of their classmates, greedy selfish Marvin Pannet, sneaking in there? Sam and Laura are determined to find out!

Dracula's Castle is Robert Swindells' third title for Yearling Books. Already available are *Room 13*, which won the 1990 Children's Book Award, and *The Postbox Mystery*, another adventure for Sam and Laura.

Also available by Robert Swindells,
and published by Yearling Books:

ROOM 13
THE POSTBOX MYSTERY

Also available by Robert Swindells in
hardcover, published by Doubleday:

HYDRA

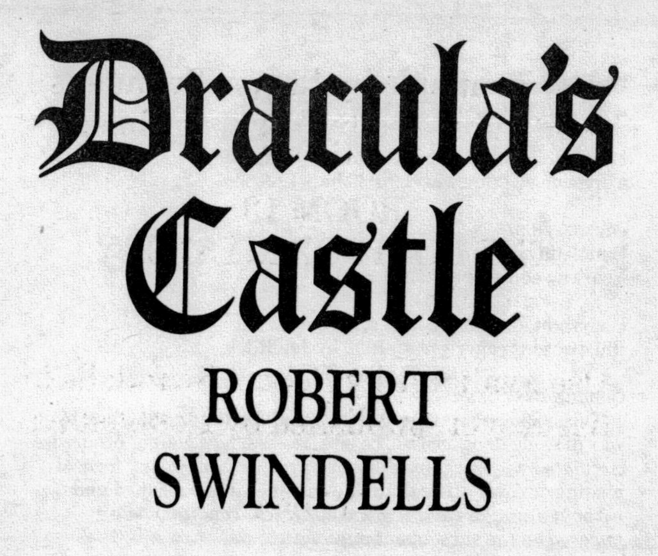

Illustrated by Jon Riley

YEARLING BOOKS

DRACULA'S CASTLE
A YEARLING BOOK 0 440 862787

First published in Great Britain by Doubleday,
a division of Transworld Publishers Ltd.

PRINTING HISTORY
Doubleday edition published 1990
Yearling edition published 1991

This book is set in 14/16pt Century Schoolbook by
Chippendale Type Ltd., Otley, West Yorkshire.

Yearling Books are published by Transworld Publishers Ltd., 61–63 Uxbridge Road, Ealing, London W5 5SA, in Australia by Transworld Publishers (Australia) Pty. Ltd., 15–23 Helles Avenue, Moorebank, NSW 2170, and in New Zealand by Transworld Publishers (N.Z.) Ltd., Cnr. Moselle and Waipareira Avenues, Henderson, Auckland.

Made and Printed in Great Britain by
The Guernsey Press Co. Ltd., Guernsey, Channel Islands.

CONTENTS

Chapter One

Dracula's Castle

Laura and Sam were twins. They were nine and a half years old, and they went to Micklefield First School in Danby. It was three-quarters of a mile from their home and there was no bus, so the twins had to walk. They didn't mind the walk, except that halfway they had to pass Dracula's Castle.

It wasn't really Dracula's Castle, of course. It was just a big empty house, but it had battlements and a tower and was surrounded by a high wall. It was a rather ugly house and nobody wanted it. Its walls were damp and mossy and the wind blew dead leaves through its broken windows. Mice made their nests in it, and at night bats flapped and twittered about the tower. If you stood between the great stone gateposts and looked in, you could hardly see

the house through the tangle of trees and shrubs gone wild. There were no gates now, but a pair of iron griffins on the gateposts seemed to snarl at passers-by, causing them to quicken their step.

Sam and Laura usually ran past Dracula's Castle. So did all the other kids. They liked to frighten one another by screaming or calling 'Look out!' just as somebody was crossing the gateway. It was all too easy to imagine something coming out of those bushes and grabbing you. It was a good, scary game, but you wouldn't want to pass Dracula's Castle alone.

One Monday morning in September, Sam and Laura were walking to school as usual. It was twenty-five past eight, and they could see the old house ahead. They were dawdling a bit, because Marvin Pannet was in front of them and they didn't want to catch him up. Marvin was the sort of boy who enjoys getting other children into trouble. His nickname was Starvin Gannet, because he was greedy and had an enormous appetite. He was spoilt and selfish and nobody liked him much.

Sam grinned at his sister. 'Hey, wouldn't it be great if Dracula came out now and grabbed him?'

'Ooh no!' cried Laura. 'I wouldn't want that to happen to anyone, Sam – not even Starvin Gannet.' She laughed. 'Anyway, he'd get turned into a vampire himself, and I don't want Marvin coming through my bedroom window at midnight, showing his fangs.'

'Ugh!' Sam shivered. 'Me neither. I never thought of that.'

When the twins reached the high wall, Marvin was approaching the gateway. He was alone as usual, but he didn't start to run or swerve on to the road as they'd expected him to. Instead he turned in through the gateway.

Sam gasped. 'What's he playing at, Laura – why has he gone in there?'

Laura shook her head. 'Dunno.' Then she smiled and said, 'Yes I do. He spotted us coming and he's hiding in the bushes, ready to jump out and scare us half to death. Listen.' She grabbed her brother's sleeve. 'Ignore him, right? When he jumps out, don't look at him. Just keep walking as if nothing's happened.'

'OK.'

They approached the gateway looking straight in front of them, determined to disappoint Marvin. They passed the first griffin. Nothing happened. They reached the middle. Still nothing. As they drew level with the second griffin Sam whispered, 'He's not there.'

They stopped and turned. Nobody was in the gateway. Nothing moved in the bushes. Marvin Pannet had disappeared.

Chapter Two

Oooh! You Little Fibber!

'David Oldroyd.'
'Here, Miss.'
'Tracy Palin.'
'Here, Miss.'
'Marvin Pannet.'

Miss Rogers waited, then looked up. 'Has anyone seen Marvin this morning?'

Sam looked across at Laura, who

shook her head. If they told Miss Rogers they'd seen him going into the grounds of Dracula's Castle, he'd be in trouble. The Head Teacher was always warning them to stay away from the old house. Old houses are dangerous, she'd say. They have loose stairs and holes in the floor. The Head Teacher knew a boy who went exploring in an abandoned house and got stuck in a hole. The fire brigade had to pull him out but his trousers

stayed in the hole and he had to walk home in his underpants.

Miss Rogers marked Marvin absent and went on with the register.

After register they did writing. Laura liked writing, but she couldn't really enjoy it this morning. Suppose Marvin had gone inside the house and got stuck in a hole?

She was just about to put her hand up when the door opened and Marvin walked in.

Miss Rogers looked at her watch. 'Marvin Pannet,' she said. 'It is twenty minutes past nine. Where have you been?'

'Please, Miss,' said Marvin, 'I was sick after my breakfast and my mum thought I should rest for half an hour.'

Oooh! You little fibber! thought Laura. She looked at Sam, who was thinking the same thing.

'And how do you feel now?' asked Miss Rogers.

'OK, thank you, Miss,' said Marvin with a brave smile. He went to his place, got out his things and began to work. Miss Rogers sighed and sat down to alter the register.

Chapter Three

There He Goes Again

'Fancy telling Miss Rogers he was sick, and all the time he was just messing about.'

It was playtime. Sam and Laura were sitting on the grass. Laura nodded. 'I know. And pretending to be so brave about it as well. "And how do you feel now?" "OK thank you, Miss." Makes you sick.'

'Mind you,' said Sam. 'He was pretty brave to go into Dracula's Castle all by himself.'

Laura shook her head. 'He probably didn't go in the house, Sam. Just the garden.'

'Yes, but still. I wouldn't go in there. Would you?'

' 'Course I would. I can do anything Starvin Gannet can do.'

'I don't believe you. You always run past, same as everybody else.'

'Right, clever-clogs. I'll prove it to you at home-time. I'll go in, and I bet you daren't come with me.'

It was ten minutes to four when the twins reached the gateway of the old house. It was a sunny afternoon and the birds were singing, but the place looked pretty spooky just the same. A gravelled drive had once led from the gateway to the front door of the house, but weeds and shrubs had grown over it until it looked like a

jungle trail. Laura gazed at it, biting her lip.

'Go on then,' taunted Sam. 'What're you waiting for?'

'Nothing.' The griffins were taunting her too, with their iron eyes. She took a deep breath and walked between the gateposts. She thought they might crash together and squash her, but they didn't.

Sam watched as his sister pushed her way into the tangle. He knew that she'd soon be out of sight and he couldn't let her go alone, so he followed her.

Laura heard him and turned. 'You don't have to come,' she said. 'I'm not scared.'

'Didn't say you were,' Sam replied. 'I want to come.'

They waded through the undergrowth until it thinned out and they could see the front door at the top of some slimy green steps.

They stopped. 'D'you think it's locked?' Sam whispered.

' 'Course it is,' hissed Laura.

'I dare you to go up and knock.'

'You go.'

'No way.'

'Well, I'm not. Come on – let's go home.'

They'd just started back when Laura grabbed Sam's sleeve and went 'Ssssh!' They stopped.

'What's up?'

'Listen!'

Sam listened. He heard a swishing, crackling noise. Something was pushing its way through the tangle, coming their way. He looked at Laura. 'W-what is it?'

'Dunno.' She looked around. A thick holly bush grew nearby. 'Quick – behind that bush.'

They'd just hidden themselves when a figure appeared, moving stealthily under the trees. Sam peered at it through the gloom and gave a sigh of relief. 'It's Marvin!'

'Sssh!' Laura pressed a finger to her lips. 'Let's see what he does.'

They held their breath as the boy passed close to their hiding place, then followed at a distance, moving as silently as possible. Marvin didn't look back, but moved through the trees and up the slimy steps. To the right of the door was a large window, its glass long since gone. With only a brief backward glance, Marvin gripped the rotting sill, pulled himself up and clambered into the house. They saw him for a moment, standing in the half-light, then he moved away from the window and was gone.

'Well,' breathed Sam. 'There he goes again.'

Chapter Four

Waste of an Ace Lunch

Marvin Pannet was famous for two things. First, he was easily the meanest, most selfish child in the school, and second, he brought the most fantastic lunches imaginable.

There were no dinners at Micklefield First School, so everybody brought a packed lunch. Most people had sandwiches, with an apple or a banana or perhaps a packet of crisps to follow. But not Marvin. His lunchbox contained things like chicken pieces, sausages on sticks, whipped-cream trifles and grapes. There was always enough food for two in Marvin's lunchbox, but he never shared. Nobody wanted to sit near him at lunchtime because the delicious smells made their mouths water.

That Tuesday lunchtime was different. Marvin had looked unwell all

morning, and when he opened his lunchbox at five past twelve he went 'Ooh-yuk!' and pushed it away. Sam and Laura were sitting nearby. Sam looked in Marvin's lunchbox, expecting to see a spider or an oily rag or a finger or something. He saw a chicken leg in golden breadcrumbs, a heap of delicious cherries and a wedge of chocolate gateau big enough to go down on your skateboard. 'What's

up?' he asked, wishing he had that cake in his own box.

'Eugh!' Marvin pulled a face, clasping his hands across his tummy. 'I feel sick, that's what's up. I can't eat a thing.'

'I'll eat it for you,' offered Sam.

'No you won't!' Marvin grabbed the box, snapped the lid on and hugged it to his chest. 'I'll save it till I feel a bit better.'

'Maybe you'd feel better,' said Laura, 'if you didn't go creeping about in empty houses.'

Marvin glared at her. 'What empty houses? I don't know what you're talking about.'

'Oh yes you do. We saw you yesterday, Sam and me. After school. You went into Dracula's Castle.'

'I did not, so there!'

'Yes you did. You got in through a window. We were watching you.'

'No you weren't. I'd have seen you.'

'How, if you weren't there yourself?'

'Well!' Marvin looked down at the table. 'It's none of your business.'

'Yes it is, Marvin. Old houses are dangerous. What if something happened to you – something awful? Sam and I would get the blame for not stopping you.'

'Well, nothing's going to happen so leave me alone.' He stood up and walked away with his lunchbox under his arm. Laura gazed after him.

'It's a waste of time talking to Starvin,' she said.

'It's a waste of an ace lunch,' muttered Sam.

Chapter Five

Rumpelstiltskin

'There are no fang holes in his neck,' said Sam. It was just after half past three and the twins were walking home, taking care to keep Marvin Pannet in sight. Marvin was dawdling along in front of them, eating from the famous lunchbox. He'd passed Dracula's Castle without going in, and the twins were passing it now.

Laura looked at her brother. 'How d'you know there are no fang holes, Sam?'

' 'Cause I had a good look while you and he were arguing at lunchtime.'

'Yes, but they might be under his collar. He was terribly white this morning, and that's one of the signs.'

Sam laughed. 'You know how greedy he is. He probably ate about four breakfasts and made himself ill. Look at him now – stuffing his face with chicken and chocolate cake. His mum'll have tea ready when he gets home, and old Starvin will groan and say he can't eat a thing. His mum'll think her little precious is coming down with the flu or something.'

Laura shook her head. 'I think something's got power over him, Sam. Why else would he go in that spooky house?'

'Perhaps there's a trifle-mine in there,' suggested Sam. 'Or a fudge-tree.'

'Ha-ha,' sneered Laura. 'Very

funny, Sam. Anyway, I'm going to mention it to Dad.'

Sam laughed again. 'I wouldn't be you, then.'

The twins' mother had gone away when they were very small, but their dad was good at looking after them. Sam and Laura looked after him too, shopping on the way home from school and having tea ready when he got in.

When the meal was over that day, Laura started to tell her father about Marvin and the old house, but he

interrupted her. 'There are no vampires, Laura,' he said. 'Dracula is just a character in a story, like Little Red Riding Hood or Tom Thumb.' He smiled. 'You'll be telling me that you met Rumpelstiltskin at the top of Elm Tree Avenue next.'

Laura tried to go on, but her father wouldn't listen. He said she'd been watching too much television and went off to have his bath.

'Well,' she sighed, as she and Sam shared the washing-up, 'that was another waste of time. Why is it grown-ups never believe anything you tell them?'

Sam shrugged. 'I knew Dad wouldn't listen. You could bring Dracula home to tea and he'd say it was the milkman. What are we going to do now?'

Laura shook her head. 'I don't know, Sam. Wait and see what happens, I suppose.'

Chapter Six

Mrs Pannet

Marvin was absent on Wednesday. Sam and Laura spent the morning looking out of the window, watching the door and glancing at each other across the room. Marvin must be in the old house again, but why? What did he do there? It had to be something pretty interesting or he wouldn't risk playing truant like this.

Sam chewed the end of his pencil. Maybe Laura's right, he thought. Maybe something has got power over Marvin. Dad says there are no vampires, but how does he know? Just because you've never seen something doesn't mean it doesn't exist. I've never seen a coconut tree but there *are* coconut trees. And why does everybody call the old house Dracula's Castle?

Laura looked at her watch. Twenty past eleven. Marvin's probably been in that house for three hours now, she thought. His mum thinks he's at school and Miss Rogers thinks he's at home. Nobody knows the truth except Sam and me. I ought to say something but I hate to tell tales and anyway, why should Miss Rogers believe me when Dad didn't? Maybe he'll turn up after lunch.

He didn't. At afternoon break Laura said, 'I'm off to Marvin's house on the way home, Sam. I've got to find out if he's ill or something.

Will you come with me?'

Sam pulled a face. 'We'll get him in terrible trouble if his mum thinks he's been at school.'

Laura nodded. 'I know, but he's mixed up in something, and the sooner his mum finds out about it the sooner it'll stop.'

They got to Marvin's house at four o'clock. Laura took a deep breath and knocked. Footsteps sounded in the hallway and Mrs Pannet opened the door.

'Laura? Sam?' She seemed surprised to see them. Laura smiled.

'We – we've come to see if Marvin's all right.'

'Oh, I see. Well, of course he was very upset at having to be sent home, but the doctor's been and he seems much better now. I'd invite you in, but he's sleeping and I don't think we ought to disturb him.' She smiled. 'It was kind of you to call.'

Laura smiled back. 'We're glad he's

all right. We'd better go now – we've got to call at the supermarket.'

'What was all that about?' said Sam, as Laura closed Mrs Pannet's gate.

Laura shook her head. 'I'm not sure, Sam. I think Marvin must've told his mum he was taken ill at school and sent home. He must've been ill because he's had the doctor, but we know it didn't happen at school.'

'I've a pretty fair idea where it did happen,' said Sam.

Laura nodded. 'Me too.' She looked at him. 'You know what we're going to have to do, don't you?'

'No.'

'You don't? Hang on a minute then, and I'll tell you.'

Chapter Seven

A Pretty Scary Plan

'We're going to have to go in there.'

Sam gulped. 'You mean inside Dracula's Castle? You and me?'

'Yes.'

'What for?'

'To find out why Marvin goes in.'

'When?'

'Straight after school tomorrow.'

Sam shook his head. 'I don't fancy

it, Laura. Can't we just tell the police?'

'Tell them what, Sam? That we think there's a vampire in the old house? They'd lock us up for being cheeky. No – we've got to find out exactly what's going on in there, and then tell them.'

They called at the supermarket for salad and potatoes, then set off home. On the way, Laura told Sam about her plan.

'We want to be there as early as possible so that we've got lots of daylight and so that the other kids don't see us going in. As soon as the bell goes, we make a dash for it. We'll leave our coats at home in the morning so we don't have to go to the cloakroom. We run all the way, climb through that window and search the place. I'll have Dad's torch with me. What d'you think?'

Sam swallowed hard. 'What do I think? I think it's a pretty scary plan, Laura. I think you're crackers. I think I'd rather eat a shovelful of black beetles than go in that house. That's what I think.'

Laura looked at him. 'Will you go with me, though?'

Sam shrugged. 'I suppose so. Can't let you do it by yourself, can I? I'll be glad when it's over, that's all.'

'Me too,' said Laura. She shivered.

Chapter Eight

Come in, Marvin

Thursday morning dawned bright and clear, and the first part of Laura's plan went perfectly. Dad always went to work before the twins set off for school, so there was nobody to say 'Take your coats – it might rain this afternoon,' or 'Why do you need a torch?' They left their coats, took the torch and locked up the house.

It was an ordinary day at school, except that Marvin was absent again. There was a note for Miss Rogers from Mrs Pannet, so the twins knew Marvin was safe at home. They had plenty of other things to think about though.

Sam couldn't concentrate on his sums. He sat making little squiggles in his book, thinking. A stake. In vampire films they always have a sharp stake and a mallet. They have

a cross too, because vampires are scared of crosses. We haven't got any of those things, he thought. All we've got is Dad's torch.

Laura played with a strand of her hair, winding it round her finger. Sam's right, she told herself. I'm crackers. Of course, I don't really believe there is anything horrible in that house, but suppose there is? What if I'm wrong and something's waiting for us?

The day dragged by. At morning break Sam said, 'Are we still doing it, Laura?' and Laura said, 'Yes.'

At lunchtime Sam said, 'Are you sure we're still doing it, Laura?' and Laura gulped and said, 'Yes.'

At afternoon break Sam said, 'Are you absolutely one hundred per cent certain we're still doing it, Laura?' and Laura said, 'Yes.'

The clock crept round to half past three. The bell rang. Sam looked across at Laura. Laura nodded. They ran.

Everybody else was miles behind when they reached the gateway. Sam stopped, but Laura grabbed his arm. 'Come on. We've got to get it done and be home before Dad. He'd go mad if he knew what we were doing.'

Sam wished his father would show up right now, before his barmy sister dragged him into the bushes, but of course he didn't. Sam shook off Laura's grip and followed her through the tangled undergrowth to the foot of the slimy steps.

'Right.' Laura rummaged in her shoulder bag and produced the black rubber torch. 'Follow me.'

'Barmy,' muttered Sam, following her up the steps. 'Crackers.'

They climbed through the window and found themselves standing on broken glass in a big, dim room. It was cold, and there was a smell like toadstools. Sam shivered and wrinkled up his nose. 'It's freezing in here,' he grumbled. 'And it stinks too.'

'What did you expect?' hissed

Laura. 'Buckingham Palace? Come on!'

Laura switched on the torch, and they followed its beam across the littered floor and out into a hallway. At one end was the door they had seen from outside. Opposite them was another door, also closed. At the far end a staircase went up into blackness.

Laura shone the torch on the closed door. 'I wonder what's in there?'

'Dunno,' croaked Sam. 'I hope it's Dad and Miss Rogers and the whole police force.'

'Don't be daft.' Laura crossed the hallway, twisted the knob and pushed. The door creaked open. She shone the torch around and something went skittering across the floor. Sam leapt back.

'What the heck's that?'

Laura shook her head 'Mouse, I expect. Or a rat. Nothing big anyway. Come on.' She made for the stairs.

Sam hung back. 'We don't have to go up there, do we?'

Laura shone the torch in his eyes. 'We haven't found anything down here, have we?'

Sam twisted his face aside and screwed up his eyes. 'I don't want to find anything, Laura. I want my tea. Let's go home.'

'No way! Not till we've looked everywhere. We're supposed to be solving a mystery – remember?'

'It's an empty house, Laura. No mystery.'

'Then there's nothing to be scared of, is there? Come on.'

The stairs creaked a lot and seemed to give under their weight. Sam imagined himself falling through into a pitch-black cellar full of monsters.

'Hey, look!' Laura had reached the top of the stairs. She was shining the torch on the floor.

Sam looked. 'What is it?'

'Footprints in the dust.'

Sam swallowed. 'Whose footprints?'

'Marvin's, of course. Look – they lead to that door.'

'I don't like it, Laura. Can't we just go – please? We haven't got a stake or a cross or anything.'

'You're a baby, Sam, d'you know that?' She left him at the top of the stairs and crept towards the door. She gripped the knob and was about to turn it when she heard a voice.

'Come in, Marvin,' it said.

Chapter Nine

Munching Time

Laura snatched back her hand. Sam, who had heard nothing, called, 'What's up?' She didn't reply, but beckoned him to join her. He crept along the landing and whispered, 'What is it?'

'Somebody said, "Come in, Marvin."'

'They didn't.'

'They did.'

'What you gonna do?'

'Dunno. D'you think I should knock?'

'Don't ask me.'

Laura knocked, timidly. At once a voice said, 'Marvin? Is that you?' Laura took a deep breath, flung the door open and shone the torch around.

It was a small, square room with a blind over its window. In the middle of the room was a large table,

piled high with fruitgums, pastilles, jelly-babies, chocolate bars, crisps and aniseed balls.

'Ooo-wow!' cried Sam. 'Look at all that grub.'

'I'm looking,' breathed Laura. 'It's like a supermarket. No wonder Marvin's been coming here.'

'Good afternoon, children.'

The voice came from a corner. Laura swung the torch. The twins saw a face with eyes screwed tight shut and a hand up to shield them.

'Would you mind pointing that thing down, or a little to one side? I'm not very fond of the light.' The speaker was sitting on a wooden chair. Laura lowered the beam and saw that he wore a black cape lined with red. He smiled, and his smile had fangs in it.

'I mean you no harm,' the vampire said.

Laura gazed at him, then at the table. 'Whose is all this stuff?'

'Yours. You found it, didn't you?

Why don't you just close that door and get stuck in before somebody else comes along?'

'Nobody'll come. And anyway, what if they did? There's enough here for a hundred people.'

'Oooh!' the vampire shivered, screwing up his face. 'Don't talk about sharing, please – it makes me feel ill.' He nodded towards the table. 'Go on. Spoil yourselves.' He chuckled. 'Think how furious your friends would be if they knew.'

Laura frowned. 'Is this what Marvin's been doing? Coming here every day, gorging himself? No wonder he's been ill. No wonder he's been off his food.'

The vampire chuckled. 'Marvin. What a gorgeous, greedy little pig that child is. How I wish he were my son.'

'It's disgusting!' cried Laura. 'We thought something awful was happening to him, and all the time he was—' She broke off and shone the light in

the vampire's eyes. 'What have you been doing to Marvin, anyway?'

The vampire turned his face aside. 'Ah, Marvin! So selfish. So wonderfully sneaky. Tell me where he is – I miss him dreadfully.'

'He's safe at home,' said Laura. 'So no more blood for you, monster.'

The vampire wrinkled up his nose. 'Blood?'

'Yes, blood. And don't pretend you don't know what I'm talking about. You're Dracula, aren't you?'

'Oh – ho-ho, I see – ha-ha-ha!' He bent forward, lifted his hand and gently moved the torch a little to one side. 'That's better.' He looked at Laura. 'You've been watching too many of those dreadful films – the ones with Christopher Lee.'

Laura gazed at him. 'Are you trying to tell us you're not Dracula?'

'It's not *Dracula*, young woman – it's *Count* Dracula. Kindly show a little respect. And no – I am not he.'

'Who are you, then?'

'Snacula, of course – Count Snacula. It's where the word "snack" comes from. Don't they teach you anything at school?'

'You mean you don't bite people's necks and suck their blood?'

'Ugh!' The vampire shuddered. 'Do you mind? Greed, that's my food. Great big helpings of greed, served with selfishness and topped off with sneakiness sauce. And for pudding, there's nothing I like more than a large dollop of unhappiness, swimming in misery.' He rubbed his hands together and licked his lips. 'The more greed there is in the world, the fatter I get.'

Laura looked down at Snacula. So that's your game, she thought. Sitting here in the dark like a big black spider, enticing children into your web. Making them selfish and greedy, then sending them out to spread greed and selfishness everywhere. Well, I think I know how to fix you, *Mister* Snacula. She smiled.

Snacula looked nervous. 'Why are you smiling? You haven't got a cross with you, by any chance?'

Laura shook her head. Snacula sighed. 'Thank goodness for that. If there's one thing I can't stand, it's a cross.'

'Why?' asked Sam.

The vampire shook his head. 'It's a long story, and you'll be wanting to get off home. In fact, I'd say you have about half an hour's munching time left.'

'We want to hear,' insisted Sam. 'Tell us.'

Chapter Ten

Snacula's Story

Snacula sighed. 'Very well. If you insist. But it's a pity. You could be cramming your hungry little tummies, you know.' He settled himself more comfortably on his chair and said, 'Once, a long time ago and in another country, there was a meeting. It was outdoors, and a long way from the shops. Thousands attended.

They'd come to hear a man speak about love, and peace, and dreadfu' stuff like that. Don't ask me why. Anyway, there they were, and it was a long meeting and people started getting hungry. There was nothing they could do about it, because there were no shops and none of them had thought to bring a picnic. None, that is, except one little boy. He had a very nice lunch with him – fish it was, and home-baked bread. Now the man who was speaking knew about this lunch, and do you know what he did?'

'What?' asked Sam.

'He persuaded the child to share it out. Five thousand people. You can imagine how much he had left for himself. Ugh! Horrible. Anyway, that man's symbol is the cross, and that's why I can't stand crosses.'

'What about parties?' said Laura. 'D'you like them?'

'Of course not!' Snacula shuddered.

'All those children sharing. All that happiness.'

'I thought not!' cried Laura. 'Well, I'll tell you what, Mister Snacula. We're going to throw a party, see? A super one. Right here and now!'

Chapter Eleven

The Party

'No!' The vampire's eyes widened with fear.

Laura nodded.

'Yes,' she hissed. 'There's kids passing by at this moment. Loads of 'em. We'll fetch them in. We'll SHARE!'

'Aaaagh!' Snacula tried to get up. Laura shone the torch in his eyes. 'Sam!' she rapped. 'Go to the gateway.

Stop the kids. Tell 'em there's a party in Dracula's Castle.' She chuckled. 'Snacula's Castle, I mean. Get them up here as fast as you can.'

As Sam went through the doorway, Laura crossed to the window and tore down the blind. Sunlight streamed in, warm and golden. The vampire screamed and curled up on the chair, his arms wrapped round his head. Moments later Laura heard excited

voices below, and footfalls on the stairs.

As children began pouring into the room, the vampire moaned and wept. He covered his face with his hands and rocked himself on the chair saying, 'There isn't enough, I tell you. You'll never make yourselves sick now, or send your teeth rotten. I told you to keep it all for yourselves.'

The children crowded round Sam,

who handed out armfuls of sweets while Laura kept a watchful eye on Snacula. One child glanced across at the weeping vampire and said, 'Who's that, then?'

'Nobody important,' said Laura. 'He'll be going soon anyway.'

She was right. Snacula was going. You could see him shrinking. Each time somebody smiled or offered a sweet to somebody else he screamed and moaned and became a little smaller. Soon, his feet no longer reached the floor, and his chin had disappeared inside his cape. His voice was becoming higher. He screamed and raged and kicked and began to look so funny that Laura couldn't help laughing.

'Don't laugh!' screeched Snacula. 'I hate to hear children laughing.' But the more he raged in his funny, piping voice, the more Laura laughed, and the more she laughed, the more he shrank. Before long there was just a cape, with two tiny feet sticking out the bottom and a reedy voice coming out of a hole in the top. Sam pointed at the little feet, drumming with rage on the edge of the seat, and collapsed laughing. There was no longer any need to guard Snacula, so Laura switched off the torch and rolled about on the floor, helpless with mirth.

Laughter is infectious, and soon all the children were laughing through mouthfuls of sweets and chocolate. What was left of Snacula's voice got drowned out by the laughter, and when Laura wiped the tears from her eyes and looked, he had disappeared completely.

Chapter Twelve

The Best Thing of All

Fridays are nearly always good because there's no school tomorrow or the next day, and you feel happy even if it's raining and you've got fishpaste sandwiches for lunch again. And if it's a special Friday, like your birthday or the start of the holidays, it's even better.

This Friday was very special for

Sam and Laura. It wasn't their birthday or the start of the holidays or anything like that. They didn't know what it was really, but they woke up feeling happy. The sun was shining, Dad was in a good mood and it was sausages for breakfast. People smiled at them on the street, and when they passed the old house the griffins seemed to smile too.

Marvin was back at school, and when Laura asked him if he was feeling better, he didn't thump her or stick out his tongue or tell her to mind her own business. Instead he smiled and said, 'I feel much better, Laura, thank you.' He looked better, too.

It was such a lovely morning that Miss Rogers decided to cancel lessons and take her class for a walk in the park. Sam was amazed. 'I don't believe all this,' he told himself. 'Something's bound to spoil it before the day's out.'

It didn't. They had a long walk, the

birds sang in the trees, and Miss Rogers even let them play on the swings for a while before taking them back to school.

It was lunchtime when they got back, and it was then that the best thing of all happened.

It was Marvin Pannet, of course. Starvin Gannet and the giant lunch-box. He opened it as usual, and as

usual it was crammed with scrumptious treats. There were about six helpings of fried chicken, a jumbo cherry pie smothered in whipped cream, a dozen little iced cakes and a mound of fresh strawberries you could just about fit on a lorry. Mouth-watering smells drifted about the room. Everybody pretended to be busy with their own lunch, but as usual Marvin's feast made their food seem poor and boring. Marvin gazed into his box then looked up, smiling.

'I hope somebody's going to help me eat all this,' he said.

THE END

ABOUT THE AUTHOR

Robert Swindells left school at fifteen and worked as a copyholder on a local newspaper. At seventeen he joined the RAF for three years, two of which he served in Germany. He then worked as a clerk, an engineer, and a printer before training and working as a teacher. He is now a full-time writer and lives on the Yorkshire moors.

He has written many books for young readers, including the winner of the 1990 Children's Book Award, *Room 13* (published by Doubleday and Yearling Books), *The Postbox Mystery* (published by Yearling Books), *Hydra* (published by Doubleday) and, for older readers, the award-winning *Brother in the Land* and *Staying Up* (published by Corgi Freeway Books). As well as writing, Robert Swindells enjoys keeping fit, travelling and reading.